E
CHI

Chin-Lee, Cynthia.

Almond cookies &
dragon well tea.

$14.95

000035643
08/10/2001

DATE			

ALMOND COOKIES & DRAGON WELL TEA

Written By Cynthia Chin-Lee

Illustrated By You Shan Tang

Library of Congress Cataloging-in-Publication Data

Chin-Lee, Cynthia
Almond Cookies & Dragon Well Tea/Cynthia Chin-Lee
illustrated by You Shan Tang

     p.   cm.

Summary: Erica visits the home of Nancy, a Chinese American
girl, and makes many delightful discoveries about her friend's
cultural heritage.

ISBN No. 1-879965-03-8: $1 .95
1. Chinese Americans -- Fiction. 2. Friendship -- Fiction]
I. Tang, You Shan, ill. II. Title.
III. Title: Almond Cookies & Dragon Well Tea.

PZ7. C4427Al   1992
[E] --dc20   92-21618
               CIP
               AC

This is a New Book, Written and Illustrated
Especially for Polychrome Books
First Edition, May 1993

Designed, produced and published by
Polychrome Publishing Corporation
4509 North Francisco Avenue, Chicago, Illinois 60625-3808
(773) 478-4455   Fax:(773) 478-0786

Email: polypub@earthlink.net
Website: www.home.earthlink.net/~polypub

Printed in China

10 9 8 7 6 5 4 3

ISBN 1-879965-03-8

To the memory of my grandfather,
to my mother,
and to my daughter, Vanessa

-Cynthia Chin-Lee

To my wife, Jian Xu

-You Shan Tang

Erica and Nancy were good friends at school. Erica's last name was Howard, and Nancy's last name was Hong, so they often got to sit next to each other in class.
Everyday they ate lunch together, and sometimes they would bring goodies like fruit or cookies to share with one another.
At recess, they played Hopscotch and Jump Rope.
Whenever they had to choose partners, they always chose each other.

One day Erica was very excited because
Nancy had invited her to visit for the first time.
Erica knew that Nancy's family originally came
from China and she wondered if Nancy's home
would be strange and different.
She hoped that she would be able to remember
her manners and behave properly.

After school, Erica walked home with Nancy.
In her bookbag she carried a small box of candy
wrapped in gold paper with a red bow
that she had helped her mother pick out
as a gift for Nancy and her family.

Nancy lived with her parents in an old brown townhouse.
The first floor was a laundry where Nancy's parents
and grandparents worked.
Nancy and her family lived upstairs.

When they arrived at Nancy's home, Nancy hugged her mother and introduced Erica to her mother.

"Welcome to our home, Erica," said Nancy's mother. Shyly, Erica held out the box of candy to Nancy and Mrs. Hong.

"How thoughtful," Nancy's mother said. "I'm sure we'll enjoy it." Erica beamed. So far, she had not forgotten any of her manners. She was beginning to feel visiting was not so strange.

Then Nancy introduced Erica to her grandparents. "Po Po," said Nancy to her grandmother, "this is my friend, Erica." Po Po smiled at Erica. "Gung Gung," continued Nancy to her grandfather, "this is Erica."

The tall, sturdy man with cloud white hair greeted Erica, "Ni hao?"

Nancy whispered to Erica, "That means, 'How are you?'"
So Erica answered him, "Ni hao." Erica and Nancy giggled.
"Now you're learning Chinese!" said Nancy.

Nancy's grandmother came from the kitchen with a tray of cookies and Chinese tea.

"These are almond cookies.
Po Po makes the best ones in town,"
Nancy boasted.

Each cookie had an almond sliver in the center
and looked like a bright yellow flower.
Erica bit into one of the crumbly, golden cookies
and agreed, "These are delicious, Po Po."

Po Po grinned when she heard that.

Next Erica took a sip of tea. What a delicious fragrance the tea had. Nancy told her, "This is Dragon Well Tea; it's special because it comes from only one place in China. The well water there is so sweet it is said to be guarded by a dragon. We serve it only to our best friends because it's so rare." The special tea and Nancy's words made Erica feel warm all over.

After they finished their tea and cookies, Nancy showed
Erica the house. Erica did not think that
it seemed too different from her own except that
in one corner of the living room stood a family altar
in a red, wooden frame.
In front of it were a bowl of oranges, a plate of almond
cookies and some incense sticks poking out of a brass burner.
Erica wrinkled her nose when she smelled the incense.

"That's how we remember our ancestors," explained Nancy.
Erica asked, "Why do you have food and incense
in front of the altar?"

"The food is for our great grandparents' spirits to 'eat.'
We burn the incense so they can smell nice things
in heaven." Erica liked the family altar;
she would suggest to her parents that they have
one to remember her Grandma Howard.

Erica noticed a musical instrument on the dining room table.
"What's this?" she asked.

"It's a Chinese zither. We call it gu zheng. Do you want me
to play it?" Nancy asked.

Erica hadn't known her friend could play a musical instrument.
She watched as Nancy plucked the strings of the zither.
Erica thought she had never heard such enchanting music.
It sounded like water rushing over the rocks in a stream.

She would have liked to listen longer,
but Nancy wanted to show her the laundry downstairs.
The laundry, where Nancy's father was hard at work,
was hot and steamy like a rain forest.
Nancy showed her the dryers that tumbled
the clothes, "barump barump" and the huge presses
that looked like long pancake griddles.
"Ssssss...," they hissed a breath of steam
when they clamped down.

Just then Nancy's father shooed them out of the laundry.
Gung Gung smiled and picked up his cane.
Without saying a word, the two girls accompanied
him to the corner drugstore across the street.

Before they entered, he placed a quarter into each of their palms. "What's this for?" asked Erica.

"It's for peanuts, so we can feed the pigeons," said Nancy.

At first Erica was a little afraid of the pigeons,
so she threw the peanuts far, making sure to
scatter them. Then, as she got braver,
she dropped the peanuts closer and closer.
She called to Nancy, "Look! The pigeons can almost eat
the peanuts out of my hand!"
Her fear of the pigeons reminded her that before she came
to visit Nancy, she had been afraid of going to a new
and strange house.
Now it didn't feel strange or different at all.

When the peanuts were all gone, they played
Hide and Seek and Red Light/Green Light.
Gung Gung watched them from a bench,
reading his Chinese newspaper and taking a quick nap.

Erica was sorry when it was dusk and Mrs. Hong came
to get them. How quickly the afternoon passed.
She was quiet as Nancy and her mother walked her home.

"You'll come and play again, won't you?" asked Nancy.

Erica brightened. "Oh, yes!" she said.

Smiling, Mrs. Hong said, "There will be plenty of visits.
Until the next time..." She handed a brown paper bag to Nancy.

Nancy gave the bag to Erica.

When Erica opened the brown paper bag, a host of pleasant memories seemed to drift into the air.
In the bag were some of Po Po's almond cookies and Dragon Well Tea.
She thanked Nancy and said "I can't wait until we can play again. I hope you'll come to my house next time."

THE END

再見，下次再来！

Founded in 1990, Polychrome Publishing Corporation is an independent press located in Chicago, Illinois, producing children's books for a muliculural market. Polychrome books introduce characters and illustrate situations with which children of all colors can readily identify. They are designed to promote racial, ethnic, cultural and religious tolerance and understanding.

We live in a multicultural world. We at Polychrome Publishing Corporation believe that our children need a balanced multicultural education if they are to thrive in that world. Polychrome books can help create that balance

Polychrome Publishing Corporation

Acknowledgments:

Polychrome Publishing Corporation appreciates the encouragement and help received from Michael and Kay Janis, Joyce MW Jenkin, Ashraf Manji and Philip Wong as well as the interest and support of the Asian American community.

Also special appreciation to Roger, Vicki and George Yamate; Laura and Mitchell Witkowski; Janet Wong; and Miguel Neri for all their efforts.

Cynthia Chin-Lee thanks the following people for their help and support: Mary and John Pan, Nancy and William Chin-Lee, Roger Dearth, Ruthann Lum McCunn, Su Ann and Kevin Kiser, Janet Bein, and Rebecca Laird.

Other books by Polychrome Publishing Corporation:

Char Siu Bao Boy   ISBN 1-879965-00-3
32 pages Hardbound (with color illustrations). Written by Sandra S. Yamate and illustrated by Joyce MW Jenkin, this story introduces us to Charlie, a Chinese American boy who loves eating his favorite ethnic food for lunch. His friends find his eating preferences strange. Charlie succumbs to peer pressure but misses eating his char siu bao. Find out how he learns to balance assimilation and cultural preservation. Recommended by the State of Hawaii Department of Education.

Ashok By Any Other Name   ISBN 1-879965-01-1
36 Pages Hardbound with paper jacket (with color illustrations). Written by Sandra S. Yamate and illustrated by Janice Tohinaka. This story is about Ashok, an Indian American boy who wishes he had a more "American" name and the mishaps he experiences as he searches for the perfect name for himself.

Nene And The Horrible Math Monster   ISBN 1-879965-02-X
36 pages Hardbound with paper jacket (with color illustrations). Written by Marie Villanueva and illustrated by Ria Unson. Nene, a Filipino American girl confronts the model minority myth, that all Asians excel at mathematics, and in doing so, overcomes her fears.

Blue Jay In The Desert   ISBN 1-879965-04-6
36 pages Hardbound with paper jacket (with color illustrations). Written by Marlene Shigekawa and illustrated by Isao Kikuchi. This is the story of a Japanese American boy and his family who are interned during World War II. It tells the story of young Junior and his Grandfather's message of hope.

ONE small GIRL   ISBN 1-879965-05-4
30 pages Hardbound with paper jacket (with color illustrations). Written by Jennifer L. Chan and illustrated by Wendy K. Lee. Do all Asian Americans look alike? Jennifer Lee is one small girl trying to amuse herself in Grandmother's store and Uncle's store next door, but it's hard when she's not supposed to touch anything. As she goes back and forth between the two stores, Jennifer Lee finds a way to double the entertainment for one small girl in two big stores.